# EMILY
## ACROSS THE
## JAMES BAY
## BRIDGE

# EMILY
## ACROSS THE
# JAMES BAY
# BRIDGE
## JULIE LAWSON

PENGUIN
CANADA

*The author wishes to acknowledge Cindy Kantor*
*for bringing her idea for this series to Penguin.*

## PENGUIN CANADA
### Published by the Penguin Group

Penguin Books, a division of Pearson Canada, 10 Alcorn Avenue, Toronto, Ontario,
Canada M4V 3B2
Penguin Books Ltd, 80 Strand, London WC2R 0RL, England
Penguin Putnam Inc., 375 Hudson Street, New York, New York 10014, U.S.A.
Penguin Books Australia Ltd, 250 Camberwell Road, Camberwell, Victoria 3124, Australia
Penguin Books India (P) Ltd, 11, Community Centre, Panchsheel Park,
New Delhi – 110 017, India
Penguin Books (NZ) Ltd, cnr Rosedale and Airborne Roads, Albany, Auckland 1310,
New Zealand
Penguin Books (South Africa) (Pty) Ltd, 24 Sturdee Avenue, Rosebank 2196, South Africa

Penguin Books Ltd, Registered Offices: 80 Strand, London WC2R 0RL, England

DESIGN: MATTHEWS COMMUNICATIONS DESIGN INC.
MAP ILLUSTRATION: SHARON MATTHEWS
INTERIOR ILLUSTRATIONS: JANET WILSON

First published, 2001

7   9   10   8   6

Copyright © Julie Lawson, 2001

Manufactured in Canada

NATIONAL LIBRARY OF CANADA CATALOGUING IN PUBLICATION DATA

Lawson, Julie, 1947–
Across the James Bay bridge : Emily
(Our Canadian girl)
ISBN 0-14-100250-6

1. Chinese—British Columbia—Victoria—History—Juvenile fiction.
I. Title. II. Series.

PS8573.A94A73 2001      jC813'.54    C2001-901159-8
PZ7.L43828Ac 2001

Visit Penguin Books' website at **www.penguin.ca**

*For*
*Charlayne Thornton-Joe*

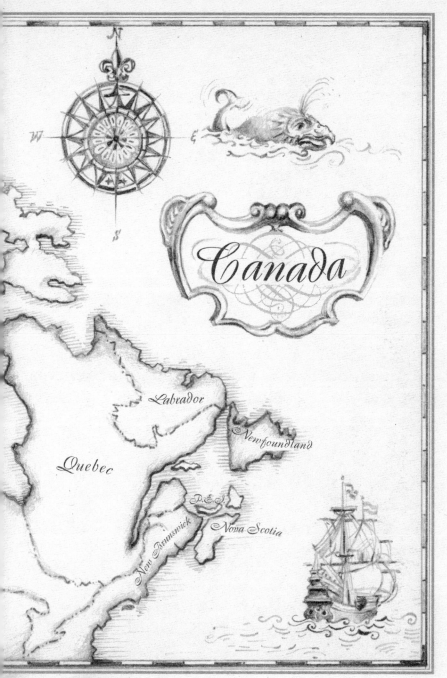

# Canada

Labrador

Newfoundland

Quebec

P.E.I.

New Brunswick

Nova Scotia

 *Marks the location of the story*

# MEET EMILY

THE YEAR IS 1896. THE PLACE IS VICTORIA, BRITISH Columbia. The young girl you're about to meet is ten-year-old Emily Murdoch.

Emily and her two younger sisters were born in the Dominion of Canada, but her parents came from England, in the 1880s. They settled in a Victoria neighbourhood called James Bay, a residential area popular with working-class, middle-class, and upper-class families. It is also an industrial area, with factories, shipyards, and an ocean dock that could accommodate large vessels.

Emily's father works in a bank, and she and her sisters enjoy a comfortable, middle-class lifestyle. Like other girls her age, Emily goes to school and church, and enjoys playing with her friends.

By 1889, Victoria was the largest and wealthiest city in the province. Its location, on the southeastern tip of

Vancouver Island, made it a commercial centre for foreign trade, and the first available seaport north of San Francisco. It housed the provincial government, the Royal Navy, and the second-largest iron-works on the Pacific coast. It was a large manufacturing centre, and boasted an assortment of activities related to forestry, fishing, sealing, agriculture, and commerce.

During Emily's ten years, the Esquimalt and Nanaimo Railway had arrived in town, electric lighting was introduced, and mail was delivered to her door twice a day—free. Recent improvements in the city water works provided residents with an abundant supply of pure water, ample for fire protection as well as domestic use. The city had a sewage system, indoor plumbing, and an expanding streetcar service.

Victoria also had a touch of the exotic. In the early 1880s, several shiploads of Chinese people were brought to British Columbia to work on the Fraser Canyon section of the new Canadian Pacific Railway. When the construction was complete, thousands settled in Victoria's Chinatown. Many found employment as cooks, servants, or gardeners in Victorian households such as Emily's.

Although Chinese New Year celebrations and funeral processions fascinated some white residents, anti-Chinese sentiments were still the rule of the day. In 1885, the federal government introduced a fifty-dollar head tax on every Chinese person entering the country, in an attempt to control Chinese immigration.

As 1896 is ushered in, the world around Emily is beginning to change. An increasing shortage of gold had led to panic in 1893 and a worldwide financial depression had followed. Emily is unaware of the effect this might have on her family. She expects life to go on as usual—with some new friends, perhaps, and new adventures. She hopes she'll get society's latest craze—a bicycle. But what does the new year really have in store for her?

*Turn the page and read on!*

CHAPTER N.º 1

*The first day of 1896 blew in with a bitter* wind and the threat of snow. In spite of the cold, Emily and her younger sister Jane were happy to be outside in Beacon Hill Park.

Things were bustling at home. Ten guests would be arriving later that afternoon for the Murdochs' annual New Year's party. A few of those guests had already sent ahead their Chinese servants to help Hing prepare the dinner, and Mother and Father were making sure that everything was perfect, down to the last detail. Because the girls kept getting in the way, Mother had sent four-year-old Amelia to bed for a nap and told Jane and Emily they could go to the park and feed the ducks—provided they dressed warmly and hurried home the instant they heard the gong.

The ducks were used to the girls' weekly offerings and quickly gathered around. But when a mob of seagulls squawked in for their share, Emily would have none of it. "Shoo!" she yelled. She ran in circles, flinging her arms in an attempt to scare them away. "This is a *duck* pond!"

"Look, Em!" Jane called out. She had several of the ducks trying to eat out of her hand. "One of them's pecking my finger."

"You chase the gulls for a while and let me feed them," Emily said, racing over to her sister. She took some grain from the small bag that Jane was carrying, moved a few yards away, then crouched down and held out two handfuls. "Here, ducks! Over here!"

"Over *here*!" Jane countered. Soon they were

deeply involved in a contest over who could attract the greater number.

Suddenly, the clamour of a gong echoed across the park.

"Oh, no!" Emily cried. "Is it that time already? Come on, Jane. We've got to go home." She scattered the remaining feed and grabbed her sister's hand.

Emily was used to Hing's gong. Before he'd started using it, she had always arrived late for lunch on school days. Hing had finally laid down the law. "I stand outside, beat gong when dinner ready," he'd said. "If you not here, you miss."

The gong outdid the clanging of the streetcar and could be heard throughout James Bay. The moment Emily heard it, she would stop whatever she was doing and run like the dickens. She didn't want to make Hing angry. If he was angry, there would be no lemon tarts!

No, the gong was not to be taken lightly—not on regular days, not on New Year's Day, and certainly not when Father was home.

Home was only three blocks from the park. But as the girls were nearing the end of the second block, Emily spotted something that made her forget the gong and come to an abrupt stop.

"Oh, Jane!"

"What?"

"See, on Sullivans' verandah? The bicycle." She leaned over the picket fence and sighed. "It's a Red Bird. That's what I wanted for Christmas."

"Maybe you'll get one for your birthday," Jane said. "It's not that far away." She gave Emily an encouraging smile and continued on home.

Emily stared at the bicycle. A birthday present? Jane could be right. Father had often said that a tenth birthday was extra special.

Another clanging of the gong tore her away. She could picture Father pulling out his watch, his foot tapping with impatience. Of course, once she had her bicycle, she would always be on time.

# CHAPTER N⁰ 2

*Father was waiting at the door, watch in hand.*
"Quickly, girls! The guests will be arriving in forty-five minutes. We want you scrubbed and polished." He smiled.

"Did you polish your gold tooth, Father?" Emily asked. "It's gleaming."

"Of course, my dear. You can't start a new year without giving everything a special shine. So off you go! And mind you don't dawdle."

"No, Father." She raced Jane upstairs to the bathroom for the required scrubbing.

Amelia, who looked as polished as a new penny, came in to supervise. "Don't forget your ears and your fingernails," she said. "Mother will check."

After their bath, they went to their room and found their best clothes neatly laid out on the bed.

Emily reached for her stockings. "Do you remember last year's party, Jane? There won't be as many people this year, but it will be even better because some *new* people are coming! They just arrived from England. Mr. Walsh works in the bank with Father. They've got one son in the Royal Navy and one son who's eleven. His name is George."

"How do you know? And you'd better hurry. I'm already dressed."

Emily put on her petticoat, then reached for her frilly white dress. "I know because they bought the house next door to Alice." Alice was Emily's closest friend.

Just then Mother came in, her silk dress swishing across the floor. "Still not ready? Oh,

Emily! You know how your father likes things to run smoothly." She fastened the mother-of-pearl buttons on Emily's dress, then turned her attention to her hair.

Emily squirmed and wriggled but at last the ordeal was over: starched dress done up, long curls brushed out, red velvet sash tied around her waist, matching ribbon in her hair. After her hands and fingernails—and ears—were examined, she had only to put on her shoes and go downstairs.

One by one the guests arrived. They gathered in both the sitting room and the parlour, chatting over glasses of punch while warming themselves by the fire.

Emily waited excitedly for the newcomer, George. She wanted to show him around the house and tell him about the school he'd be attending once the holidays were over. But when he and his parents arrived, there wasn't time. Dinner was announced. The guests made their way into the dining room in a leisurely fashion and took their places at the long table.

Mother had seated George and Emily side by side.

"Your neighbour, Alice, told me all about you," Emily said.

George gave her a mischievous grin. "Her brother, Tom, told me all about *you*."

"Oh, no!" Emily giggled and hid her face so he wouldn't see her blushing.

After Father said grace, Hing brought in the plates and began to serve, helped out on this occasion by a neighbour's housemaid. The first course was oyster pie, followed by a clear soup. Then came chicken and tongue and cold boiled ham, with mixed pickles and celery, onions in cream sauce, and two types of potatoes: sweet potatoes with brown sugar, mashed potatoes with gravy. Emily noticed that George was tucking in heartily, but she was careful to save room for dessert.

Finally Hing brought in the flaming plum pudding. Emily savoured every bite, especially the hard sauce poured over top.

It was a long time to sit minding your manners. Emily didn't realize how much she'd been fidgeting until she caught Father's eye. She immediately stopped pleating her linen napkin and folded her hands in her lap. She glanced at Mother, hoping to be excused from the table, but Mother shook her head and mouthed the word "toasts."

The dreaded toasts. Emily sighed loudly and slumped in her chair, prompting another stern look from Father.

Then, at last, Father was on his feet, wineglass in hand. "The Queen!" he said. Everyone stood up, raised his glass, and repeated, "The Queen!"

Emily and George were over eight years old, so they were each given a half glass of white wine. George downed his in one gulp, then made a spectacle of himself by coughing. Emily knew better— the stuff tasted horrid—so she merely touched the glass to her lips and pretended to drink.

No sooner had the Queen been toasted than Mr. Walsh stood and proposed a toast to their hostess. Once again everyone stood and raised his glass, this time to Mother. Then it was Father's turn. Stand, raise glass, sit down. Happy New Year, good health .... And so it went, round the table, with toasts to everyone.

Emily wished she could propose a marmalade instead of a toast. A marmalade to Jane and Amelia. Or why not to George? She glanced at him and stifled a giggle. With his reddish-brown hair, perhaps she ought to propose a strawberry jam!

The toasts dragged on. At last, when Emily had had all the stands and sits she could take, Father allowed the children to be excused.

"We're going to play Happy New Year with our dolls," Jane said.

"You can play, too, Em," said Amelia. "And George can make the toasts."

Emily shook her head. "We're going to have a tour of the house."

She grabbed George's hand, taking him very much by surprise, and they made their getaway up the staircase.

She proudly showed him the new bathroom, with its indoor flush toilet and claw-foot tub. Next came the play room, where her sisters' dolls were sitting down to their New Year's feast. After a quick peek inside her parents' bedroom, they went into the room Emily shared with her sisters. It was large and bright with a window seat that overlooked the street.

"I can watch everything from here," she said. "I can see when my friends are coming, and the postman and the milkman. And what the Chinese peddlers are selling."

"Chinese peddlers?" George turned up his nose.

"Haven't you seen them? They balance a bamboo pole on their shoulders and hang a basket at each end. They go from house to house all over Victoria. Some of them sell vegetables or fish, and some collect the laundry. I can watch the streetcar, too. It's electric! It goes right down our street and stops at the next block.

Wait till you hear it! The bell clangs and the over-head wires whistle and the conductor shouts hello to everyone. It takes you anywhere in the city for five cents."

Back on the main floor, they looked into the kitchen, where the Chinese servants were washing the dishes. One man paused above a vat of boiling water and caught sight of Emily.

"Em-ry!" he called out. "*Gung hey fat choy.*"

"*Gung hey fat choy!*" she replied. "That's Hing," she told George. "He's teaching me some Chinese."

George grunted. "Don't tell me you understand that *hey choy* nonsense."

"It's what the Chinese say for Happy New Year. But their new year is different from ours."

"What's 'Em-ry,' then?"

"My name, silly! He calls Alice 'A-ris.'"

"Barbarians," George muttered.

"Didn't you have a Chinese servant in England?"

George gave her a horrified look. "We had English servants, of course."

"What's in this room?" He stopped before a door at the end of the hall.

"That's Father's study. We're not allowed in unless—George!"

He was already inside, gazing at a vast collection of objects displayed in a large glass cabinet. "What's all this?"

"Father's antiquities," Emily explained. "They're from the Far East. Father got some on his travels and some were gifts. See the vase with the dragon?" She pointed to a blue-and-white porcelain vase. "It only just arrived. My uncle in London sent it. Father says it's eight hundred years old."

"Is that a real dagger beside it?" George asked. "I say! It looks like a ram's head on the handle. Can I have a closer look?"

"No!" Emily cried in alarm. "What are you doing? You can't touch it!" She reached out to stop him. As she did so, her arm brushed the vase and sent it crashing to the floor.

"Oh, no!" she gasped. Her stomach churned.

What would Father say?

"I don't think anyone heard," George said. "Do you?"

"I don't know." Her mouth felt so dry she could hardly speak.

"At least *I* didn't break it," George went on. "You're in for it now. Would you like me to tell your father? Might make it easier."

She shook her head, wishing she could die on the spot.

"Suit yourself," George said. "Shall we go back upstairs and spy on your sisters?" Before she could answer, he was gone.

With shaking fingers, Emily picked up the broken pieces. Part of the vase was still intact. If it were facing out . . . She propped it on the shelf and hid the other pieces in behind. It looked a little tippy, but it would have to do for now. Tonight she would not pray for a bicycle. She would pray that Father stay out of his study for a very long time.

She left the study and closed the door. As

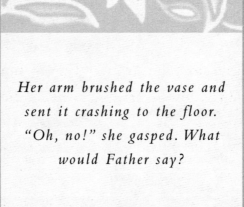

*Her arm brushed the vase and sent it crashing to the floor. "Oh, no!" she gasped. What would Father say?*

she was passing the dining room she heard her father say, "A toast—to better times."

Emily couldn't help but agree.

Then Father continued, "Not to put a damper on the festivities, but I cannot help worrying about this economic slump and its outcome. I fear we may have some tough times ahead."

Emily frowned. The broken vase certainly meant tough times for *her* once Father found out. But what did "tough times" mean for him and his guests? He worked in the bank, so perhaps it had to do with money. And if *that* were the case, maybe that was why she didn't get a bicycle for Christmas.

No, that couldn't be right. Father had no end of money. Like Jane said, he was saving the bicycle for her birthday. The thought made her smile . . . until she remembered the vase.

And later, when everyone was joining hands and singing "Auld Lang Syne," Emily had but one thought: How could she put it back together?

# CHAPTER N° 3

*As luck would have it, it snowed overnight.*
Father shovelled the verandah steps and then left
right away for his usual walk to the bank. Mother
went outside with Jane and Amelia to help them
build a snowman. Emily stayed inside. With Hing
having the day off, she had the house to herself.

She had a plan, but she had to act quickly. First
she needed glue. What kind of glue worked with
porcelain? Surely not the ordinary paste she used
for paper. She needed something strong, something hard. . . . Mother's hard sauce! Mother

often made glue with flour and water but it was lumpy. The sauce was smooth. And when it was dry it went hard, like frosting on a cake.

She dashed to the kitchen and flipped through the pages of her mother's book, the *Household Companion*, until she found the recipe. Butter, powdered sugar, brandy. She put some sugar in a bowl, added the butter, and beat it into a thick, smooth paste.

She couldn't find the brandy, but she figured a colourless liquid labelled "alcohol" would do the trick. She stirred in a few drops. The smell was so horrid she decided not to taste it. Besides, her sauce was not for pudding.

She hurried into the study and removed the broken vase. There were about ten pieces, and some were rather large. Taking one piece at a time, she applied the glue to the broken edges. Then, with trembling fingers, she fit the pieces together.

She was wiping away the smudges when she heard her sisters calling at the back door. "Emily, get us a carrot! Our snowman needs a nose! And Mother says to hurry!"

"Coming!" she cried. She returned the vase to the cabinet and gave it one last look. The blue lines of the dragon matched up, and the glue appeared to be holding. Unless Father examined the vase closely, he would never know.

The snow kept Emily's mind off the vase and her father out of his study. Victoria didn't get much snow, and Emily couldn't miss the opportunity to go sledding with her friends. As for Father, as soon as he got home from work, he took the whole family to Beacon Hill Park for sleigh rides with friends and neighbours. For two afternoons and evenings the streets rang with sleigh bells instead of the clanging streetcars.

On the third night of the new year, Emily was awakened by a dreadful shaking. The whole house rocked. Windows rattled and glassware jingled. When the shaking finally stopped, Mother and Father rushed in to calm the frightened girls.

"It was an earthquake," said Father. "It's all over now."

The next day they learned that the earthquake had lasted fifteen seconds and had been felt throughout Victoria. "It was quite severe," Father told them, "but there was no serious damage."

Emily thought of the vase. If it were discovered now, they could blame the earthquake. "Did anything get broken?" she asked. "Any dishes or . . . vases?"

"Not so much as an egg cup," Mother said. "The only thing that shattered was our nerves."

"Not even the slightest crack?" Emily persisted.

Father ruffled her hair. "What a worrier you

are! There wasn't the tiniest splinter."

"Our snowman got broke," Amelia said glumly.

"You can blame that on the rain," Father said. "There'll be no sleigh rides today."

Jane sniffed. "And no more snow."

"But there might be another earthquake?" Emily tried to keep her voice from sounding too hopeful.

"No, dear." Mother gave her a hug. "You'll sleep peacefully tonight."

# CHAPTER Nº 4

*"Go on, Emily!" George gave her a poke.*
"Sneak up and pull his pigtail."

From her hiding place behind the hedge in front of George's house, Emily watched the peddler jog-trotting along the muddy street. He was a familiar sight, dressed in dark, baggy trousers, a loose-fitting jacket, and a wide-brimmed hat. And like the other Chinese men, he wore his hair in a long pigtail.

"He's not going to bite you," Alice said. "George pulled a peddler's pigtail yesterday.

Tom and I did too."

"We dare you," George went on. "If you're not too much of a scaredy-cat."

Emily frowned. She didn't want to do it. If Hing found out, he wouldn't like it one bit.

Still, she didn't take dares lightly. And as for being a scaredy-cat? They'd see about that.

She ran up behind the peddler and gave his pigtail a good hard tug. He whirled around and shouted as she fled back to the hedge.

"He sure looked mad." Alice laughed. "Did you see him shaking his fist? He probably put a curse on you."

"Where does he live?" George asked.

"In Chinatown, where else?" said Alice. "Mother says it stinks to high heaven of sharks' fins and rotten eggs."

"You must mean thousand-year-old eggs," Emily said. "They're not really that old, and they're not rotten. They're preserved. They're dark purple on the outside and green inside."

"How do you know?" said Tom.

"Hing brought me one to taste. It was good."

The others groaned with disgust. "You wouldn't catch me eating that rubbish," George said. "And I'd never set foot in Chinatown."

"Me neither," said Alice. "Would you, Em?"

"Yes!" Emily suddenly felt very bold. "In fact, I think I might go this very afternoon. And I dare all of you to come with me."

"You can't be serious," said Tom.

"Why not? I went once before, with Father. And it's not as bad as you make out. So . . . I double dare you."

Alice shook her head. "Our parents would never allow it."

"They wouldn't need to know," Emily continued, warming to her plan. "We'll ask if we can go across the bridge into town. We could even do some errands and get candy at the grocer's." When the others still hesitated, she burst out, "You're brave enough to pull a peddler's pigtail but you won't even go to Chinatown? You only have to stay a minute. I triple dare you!" She glared at George. "If you don't, I'll tell Father you went snooping into his room. When *I* told you not to!"

George rolled his eyes. "Oh, very well. Let's all go. It might be a lark. If we remember to plug our noses."

Everyone received permission for the trip to town, and shortly after lunch they were ready to go. Mother told Emily to be back for tea and to bring home some candy for her sisters. "Behave yourself," she said. "And stay on the boardwalks. The roads are a frightful mess."

A brisk walk down Birdcage Walk led them to the wooden bridge that spanned James Bay. As they stepped onto the bridge, Emily pulled a face. "Eugh! Low tide!"

"It stinks here all the time," said Alice.

A stream of foam came spewing out of the soap-works factory on the far shore. It floated onto the mud flats and mingled with the garbage and debris that people often dumped in the bay.

"I like it at high tide," said Emily. "In the summer, Father rents a rowboat and takes us under the bridge."

Once they crossed the bridge, they headed up Government Street. Horse-drawn hacks stood one behind the other, waiting for fares. The streetcar whistled by at a good ten miles an hour.

They passed the Bank of B.C. where Emily's father worked, several dry-goods stores, a clothier's, a butcher's, and the post office. When they reached the grocer's, they hurried inside for their candy. Everything was out in the open, from hams and bacon to barrels of English biscuits and enormous rounds of cheese. Emily counted out a penny's worth of lemon barley sugar sticks and butter taffy drops, making sure she had enough for her sisters.

They left the grocer's and continued up the street. But as they were crossing the Johnson Street ravine, they heard a series of explosions that stopped them in their tracks.

"That sounds like firecrackers!" George exclaimed. "Where are they coming from?"

"Chinatown," Emily said. "We're almost there."

They reached the end of the footbridge, walked a short distance in the mud, then turned into Chinatown.

The street was crowded with Chinese people, chatting in small groups or hurrying along with their bamboo poles. A string of firecrackers, tied in tight red clusters, hung from a wooden balcony all the way down to the boardwalk below. Someone had lit the string at the lower end, and the fire was steadily popping its way to the top.

"Let's take the rest!" said George. "We can set them off in the park!" He grabbed the string and yanked it from the balcony. Then he stamped out the fire, scooped up the unlit firecrackers, and ran off.

"Stop!" someone shouted. Several men gave chase.

"Down here!" Emily cried. She ducked into a narrow brick alley, assuming the others were close behind. But when she stopped for breath, she found she was alone. Where were they? Surely they wouldn't have run off and left her.

She continued down the alley, not daring to return to the street with all the shouting going on. That George! she thought angrily. It's his fault. If I have to go home by myself . . .

The alley had begun to twist and turn, with numerous paths branching off in different directions. Emily followed one after another. Finally, with no end in sight, she realized she would have to retrace her steps.

"I hope you're satisfied, George!" she fumed. "Mr. Know-it-all!" Then anxiously, "How do I get out of here?"

Just then, who should appear but Hing.

"Em-ry?" He frowned. "What are you doing here?"

"Oh, Hing!" Her words came out in a rush. "I didn't want to pull his pigtail but they dared me. So then I dared them to come to Chinatown, especially that George, who's always getting into trouble. First it was Father's study and the vase—and it was *his* fault I broke it! And then he stole the firecrackers. That's why we ran off. I came down the alley to hide—" A thought struck her. "Is it Chinese New Year already? Is that why there are firecrackers?"

"No, no. New Year next month. Firecrackers for open new store. To scare away evil spirits and bring good fortune."

"Oh." She gave him a worried look. "Why aren't you still at my house?" He'd been there that morning, cooking the traditional Saturday roast so they could have cold pork on Sunday. "Your half day is Sunday, isn't it? Are you sick?"

"No, no. Change half day, one time. Today—" His words were interrupted by a loud banging. "Come!" He took her hand and led her back to the street.

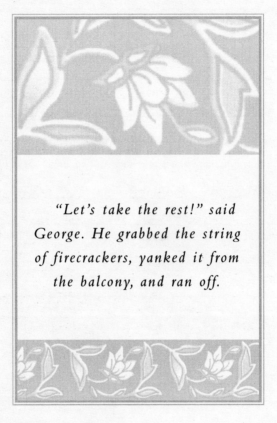

*"Let's take the rest!" said George. He grabbed the string of firecrackers, yanked it from the balcony, and ran off.*

A large and noisy procession was moving through Chinatown. Cymbals crashed. Women cried and wailed. They even held bowls under their eyes to catch the tears.

"What kind of parade is that?" Emily asked. "And why are all those people wearing white?"

"Funeral," Hing said. "Friend from home village." He told Emily he'd take her as far as the James Bay bridge, but then he would join the procession himself.

By the time they turned down Government, the street was lined with curious onlookers.

"There's Alice, up ahead," Emily said. "And Tom and George. Thank goodness, he doesn't have the firecrackers any more." She handed Hing a butter taffy drop and ran to join her friends.

# CHAPTER N.º 5

*At school on Monday, Emily was faced* with a barrage of questions. "Where's your bicycle?" her classmates asked. "You said you were getting one for Christmas."

"It's going to be a birthday present," she told them.

"How do you know for sure? What kind are you getting? Will you let us ride it sometimes?"

She answered the questions as best she could, until, much to her relief, her teacher rang the bell.

As she was walking home at noon, she once again spotted the Red Bird bicycle. This time, it was leaning against the side of the Sullivans' house.

No one was about. She went over to the bicycle and touched the smooth frame. She spun the pedals and gripped the handlebars. She clambered onto the leather seat, bracing herself against the wall. Even though her feet didn't quite reach the pedals, she closed her eyes and pretended she was flying along Dallas Road with the sea breeze in her hair. It was one of the Ten Commandments not to covet anything that belonged to a neighbour, but oh, how she coveted that bicycle! Only three weeks until her birthday. Maybe Father had already bought her bicycle. Maybe he was hiding it in the bank, away from prying eyes.

When her imaginary ride was over, she hopped off and daringly rang the little bell attached to the handlebars. Its brassy tinkle reminded her that she hadn't heard Hing's gong.

She gave the bicycle one last pat and hurried on, thinking she was either very early or extremely late.

At home, she was astonished to find her sisters bickering in the breakfast room, her mother in a panic in the kitchen, and no meal in sight.

"Emily, where have you been?" Mother cried.

Without waiting for an answer, she thrust a plate of cold tongue sandwiches into Emily's hands. "Put this on the table and come back for the milk. It never rains but it pours. Today of all days, with guests coming for tea."

"It's not raining!" Amelia squealed. "Mother, you said it was raining and pouring!"

"Hush, Amelia, and eat! You, too, Jane. And Emily, you're going to be late for school."

Between mouthfuls, Emily said, "I saw a Red Bird bicycle on my way home. I hope I get the same kind for my birthday. I sat on the seat to try it out and it was almost my size. It was rather high, but I don't think it's all that difficult to lower the seat. Won't it be grand, Mother? I'll never be late, and Hing won't ever have to bang the gong again. Where is he, anyway?"

"Oh, Emily! I'm so sorry, I know how fond you are of Hing—"

"Mother, what's happened? Is he all right?"

"When's he coming back?" Jane asked.

"Hing's hurt!" Amelia began to cry.

"No, no, it's nothing like that," Mother said reassuringly. "Girls, your father dismissed Hing this morning. He acted in haste, and I'm sure he'll regret it and make amends, but meanwhile—oh, Amelia, let Jane pour your milk, you're going to knock it over—meanwhile, the ladies will be here sharp at two o'clock and nothing's prepared!"

Emily had never seen her mother in such a state. "I'll stay home and help," she offered.

"Me too!" said Jane. "If Emily misses school, can I?"

"No, Jane."

"That's not fair!" Jane pounded the table and knocked over her milk.

"Now look what you've done! Emily, give me a hand, please."

The next several minutes were filled with crying and confusion. But soon Amelia was in bed for a nap and Jane was on her way back to school. Mother mixed batter for scones. And after clearing the table and wiping the spilt milk, Emily was set to work making egg salad sandwiches.

"What about Hing?" she asked as she sliced the bread. "Will he be here tomorrow? He promised he'd make lemon tarts tomorrow. Why did Father dismiss him? Mother—"

"Emily, please! It's all very distressing, and I'll explain in due course, but now is simply not the time. Oh, dear, look at the bread! We want thin straight across, not sloping. And for goodness' sake, don't slice your finger."

Before long, the thick-and-thin sandwiches were on a plate, the scones were in the oven, and the guests were sipping tea in the parlour.

Emily was filling a cut-glass bowl with strawberry preserves to go with the scones when she heard Hing's name. Curious, she crept down the hall and, sucking on a spoonful of preserves, put her ear to the parlour door. She was just in time to hear her mother say, ". . . discovered it broken and dismissed him this morning."

Emily gasped in disbelief. Hing could not have been dismissed because of the vase. He knew that *she* was responsible. Surely he would have said something.

"The blue and white porcelain vase," her mother went on. "Yesterday afternoon, before we went to the church social, I asked Hing to do a thorough cleaning in Robert's study. There's been the most peculiar smell of rubbing alcohol. Well, as he was cleaning the shelves in the display case, he must have dropped the vase."

"You can't trust them." Emily recognized the voice of George's mother, Mrs. Walsh. "I know it's the custom in Victoria, but I certainly wouldn't have a Chinaman in my house."

"But he's an excellent servant!" Mother exclaimed. "Ten years he's been with us, since

Emily was a baby, and not a speck of trouble."

"What did he have to say for himself?"

"Nothing. He remained absolutely silent."

Emily's stomach lurched. Hing had been dismissed because of her, and he hadn't let on . . .

"Who else could it have been?" Mother continued. "The girls are forbidden to go into the study."

"You should have hired an English servant from the start," Mrs. Walsh said. "They're much more reliable."

"Nonsense!" someone retorted. "Not any of the girls I've had. They stay for a month, then they're off getting married. No, the Orientals are definitely the best, provided you train them properly and keep an eye on them. I was saying the other day . . . excuse me, Anne, I don't mean to be rude, but is something burning?"

"Oh, mercy!" Emily bolted back to the kitchen, her mother close behind. She flung open the oven door and gagged as smoke billowed into the room. Then she grabbed the oven mitts and pulled out the blackened mess. There would be no scones served with thick cream and strawberry preserves today.

"Whatever were you thinking?" Mother spoke sharply, but sounded more exasperated than angry.

Emily tried to keep her voice from trembling. "Mother, I'm sorry. I promise I'll clean up, but right now I have to go back to school because I've forgotten something important."

"Your father will hear about this!"

"I know," Emily said as she grabbed her coat and ran out. "And I'll explain everything."

First, she had to find Hing.

# CHAPTER N.º 6

*Emily's plan was simple. She would go to* Chinatown, find Hing, and take him home with her. Once Father learned the truth about the vase, he'd likely give Emily a sound thrashing— but at least he'd give Hing back his job.

When she got to Chinatown, she turned down the same alley she'd gone into before, found the same lane, and recognized the spot where Hing had unexpectedly appeared. The problem was, where exactly had he come from?

It was different in this hidden part of

Chinatown. There were chicken coops, barking dogs, lines of washing, and gardens with winter vegetables. The tightly packed buildings bulged in on each other, sometimes three storeys high.

She walked through a courtyard and down another alley, only to reach a dead end. She tried a different route but ended up in another courtyard.

Passersby gave her curious looks. "Hing?" she asked. "Do you know Hing?" No one could help.

With a growing sense of panic, she wandered through the maze, from dead end to dead end, one courtyard to another. There were too many staircases, too many doorways. Faces peered out of windows, smoke rose from chimneys. Inside the squalid rooms, lamps were being lit. It would soon be dark. And it was starting to rain.

Just then, a peddler stepped out of a doorway. Emily was about to approach when she recognized him as the man whose pigtail she had pulled. She shuddered. She couldn't ask *him* for help. He'd think she was up to more mischief and put another curse on her. If he so much as saw her . . .

She turned too quickly, stumbled over a heap of refuse, and fell onto a jagged pile of bricks. "Oh, mercy!" A sob welled up in her throat. It was raining hard now, the wind cut through to her bones, and her hands and knees smarted horribly.

"Em-ry?"

The familiar voice made her giddy with relief.

"Oh, Hing, I'm so sorry! That vase . . . I should have told Father right away instead of trying to hide it, and now you've lost your job. So will you come home with me? I'll tell Father and he'll hire you back—" A dreadful thought struck her. What if Hing had taken another position? What if he didn't want to come back? She burst into tears. "Oh, please!"

"Come." He led her to a door a few steps away and ushered her inside a cramped and dingy room. After clearing a space for her to sit down, he poured her a cup of tea. "Drink," he said.

"Then we go home and explain."

She thanked him, then picked up the cup and frowned. The tea didn't look like proper tea; there were leaves floating on top. But she remembered her manners and took a sip. It had a slightly bitter, but pleasant taste, and it warmed her right through.

"Green tea," Hing said. "You like?"

"Yes. Thank you." As she drank the tea, she took in her surroundings—the rough pieces of furniture, a wood stove, shelves with cracked and mismatched china. On a crate beside the narrow bed she noticed a studio portrait of a young Chinese woman seated with two small boys.

"Who are they?" she wondered.

"Wife and sons." Hing smiled proudly.

"Are they in Victoria too?"

Hing's expression changed. He told Emily how he'd come to Canada in 1883 to work on the railway, hoping to earn enough money to send for his family. Two years later he'd succeeded. He'd then returned to China and spent many

*Hing told Emily how he'd come to Canada, hoping to earn enough money to send for his family.*

months visiting friends and relatives and telling them about the land they called Gold Mountain.

It was difficult to follow everything he said. He spoke slowly and all his *l*'s came out as *r*'s. But his story fascinated Emily. It was like a fairy tale, only real. Even though there was no happy ending. Hing and his family had packed their belongings for Gold Mountain only to discover that the government in Canada had established a head tax. Every Chinese entering the country had to pay fifty dollars. Hing could only afford to pay for himself.

The opportunities in Gold Mountain were so much greater than those in his homeland, he had left his wife and sons and returned to Victoria. He'd promised to send for them as soon as he could save enough money to cover their head tax.

"You must miss them," said Emily.

"I have daughter, too," he said sadly. "Born in Year of Dog. Ten years old. Like you."

"*Almost* ten," Emily reminded him. "Is she pretty, like your wife?"

"I never see her. No picture. But I think yes, she very pretty."

Emily didn't understand why Hing, who'd been working in Victoria for ten years, still hadn't saved enough money to send for his family. It would be rude to ask, but she couldn't help but wonder.

"Getting late," Hing said. "We go now."

Emily thought about his story all the way home. To think Hing had a wife and children she'd never even heard about . . . He must miss them dreadfully. And to leave Emily's cozy house, night after night, for that horrid little room . . .

She wondered if her parents knew. Well, as soon as the vase business was settled and Hing was back at work, she'd tell them. And when Father learned how lonely Hing was, he'd pay him a higher wage. Then Hing would be able to bring his family to Canada and the story would have a happy ending. Especially when Hing saw his daughter for the very first time.

## CHAPTER 7

*Father did not look pleased when Emily* came into the house. He held out his pocket watch and said sternly, "Do you see what time it is? Mother and I have been frantic. What do you have to say for yourself?"

Emily glanced over her shoulder at Hing, waiting in the doorway. Then she bowed her head and stammered, "I had to find Hing, Father. He got fired because of me. Because I broke the vase. And I was afraid to tell you."

Her parents looked at her with shocked

expressions. Before they could say anything, she rushed on.

"It was at the New Year's party and George went into your study and he wanted to see the dagger. I tried to stop him . . ." She swallowed hard to force back the tears. "I knocked over the vase and I glued it back together. Then Hing got blamed and you sent him away, and the whole time he never said it was me, even though he knew. Oh, please, Father! Please hire him back! He's got a whole family in China and a little girl—"

"That's enough for now, Emily," Father said. "Wait for me in the study. Mother and I will speak to you shortly."

The list seemed endless. Emily stood before her

father, head hung in disgrace, as Mother gave a full account of the day's disasters.

"I left her with the simple task of keeping an eye on the scones. Instead, she left the kitchen and dripped strawberry preserves on the carpet. Then she stepped in it and tracked it down the hall. The scones were burnt to cinders. And what does she do then? She flies out with a story about forgetting something at school. As for the rest! Going into the study, breaking the vase—admittedly, it was an accident—and failing to say anything . . ." Mother shook her head.

Father sighed. "You did a great wrong by not telling us about the vase. But you've put things right in an admirable way. Except for the mess in the hall and kitchen, and you'll clean that up tomorrow." He then sent her sobbing to her room.

"Don't cry, Em," Jane said, giving her a hug. "Father won't stay mad for long, and you'll still get your bicycle. And—don't tell, but I was listening outside the door and I know Hing's coming back first thing tomorrow."

Emily squeezed Jane's hand. The thought of Hing in his lonely room, with no family close by for comfort, made her cry even harder.

The next evening, Emily decided to put another plan into action.

"Father," she said, "when you and Mother came to Canada did you pay a head tax?"

"Head tacks?" Amelia looked puzzled. "That would hurt."

"Not those tacks," Emily said. "Tax like what you pay. Isn't that right, Father? Did you have to pay it?"

"What? I'm sorry, dear. What did you say?"

She repeated the question.

"Englishmen paying a head tax? Certainly not!"

"Oh. But . . . I heard people had to pay fifty dollars to come into Canada."

"Only the Chinese."

"Will they always have to pay the fifty dollars?"

"Hmm? Oh. The fifty dollars. No . . ."

Emily's face lit up. Wait till she told Hing!

Then Father continued, "It's very likely the head tax will be raised to one hundred dollars. Possibly for the best. There's enough unemployment as it is."

Oh, no. Hing would have to act quickly or pay an even higher tax.

"Father, I was wondering if you could—"

"Hush, Emily!" Mother said. "Can't you see your father's tired? You girls may be excused."

Emily sighed. Her request for Hing's raise would have to wait.

*"Happy birthday, Em!" Jane and Amelia* pounced on their sister. She kissed them both and ran downstairs to the breakfast room.

"Happy birthday, dear." Father ruffled her hair. "How does it feel to be ten years old?"

"It feels grown up! Enough to cycle around the world."

Mother laughed. "You'll have to wait another few years for that. Meanwhile, sit down and eat your breakfast. Father has a surprise."

"Yes, indeed," he said. "I want you to walk to

the bank with me this morning."

"The whole way?" She often accompanied him as far as the James Bay bridge, but going all the way to the bank was unusual.

"Yes, my dear." He flashed his gold tooth in a smile. "The whole way."

Emily looked at her parents' faces and knew that she was right. Her bicycle had to be at the bank.

But it wasn't a bicycle that awaited her.

"Here you are, Emily," Father said. "Your very own passbook. This is your account number, and you can see that I've started you off with five whole dollars."

Emily managed a smile. She mustn't appear ungrateful. Besides, it was early yet. The bicycle would likely appear at supper, along with her birthday cake and other presents.

"Where's your bicycle?" Alice asked when Emily arrived at school. "You said you were getting one for your birthday."

"It's coming later," she said.

"That's what you said at Christmas," Tom pointed out. "And you still haven't got it."

"You're not really getting a bicycle at all, are you?" George said. "You're just putting on airs. Father says they're very dear. But even so, I'm sure to get one this summer."

Emily tossed her head. "Well, I'm sure to get one this afternoon."

After school she searched her yard, the wood-shed, and the verandah. A search inside, from attic to cellar, yielded nothing. But the day was far from over.

After supper Hing brought out the birthday cake. Emily closed her eyes, made the same wish she'd been making all year, and blew out the candles. Then Mother brought in her presents. A blue velvet dress. An album for photographs. And something rolled up in brown paper and tied with string.

"Open it, Em!" Jane squirmed with excitement as Emily unrolled the paper. "It's your wish come true."

When Emily saw Jane's gift, her eyes brimmed with tears. It was a drawing of a bicycle, every detail perfect, right down to the bell on the handlebars. Beside it was a smiling little girl meant to be Emily.

"I sketched it in my art class before Christmas," Jane said. "Do you like it?"

"I love it, Jane. I'll hang it in our room straight away." She gave her a hug, then ran upstairs so Jane wouldn't see her crying.

A short time later, Father came in. He patted Emily's shoulder, then took the drawing and tacked it above the bed.

"I know you had your heart set on a real bicycle," he said. "But do you remember our New Year's party, and how we had fewer guests than usual? And how we didn't have a turkey? Well, the fact is, money is rather tight at the moment. As soon as things get better, I promise you'll have your bicycle."

Emily sniffed sadly. "Even if I'm very old, like sixteen?"

"Even if you're a grouchity old thing like me."

"You're not all that grouchity, Father."

He smiled, then reached for his handkerchief and wiped away her tears. "You know, Hing tells me that in a few days it's Chinese New Year. Would you like to go to Chinatown and see the celebration?"

"Oh, yes!" She grinned. "And since it's a new year, you'll have to polish your gold tooth."

"That's my girl! Now, let's go down and finish your cake."

Before going downstairs, Emily patted her bicycle picture and made a wish for better times.

*At breakfast on the morning of Chinese* New Year, Hing gave Emily two red scrolls decorated with tiny mirrors, paper flowers, and multicoloured tassels. "Hang on bedposts. Keep away bad spirits. Good luck for three little girls, all year. This year," he went on, "is Year of Monkey."

"In China, does every year have a different animal?" Emily wondered.

"Oh, yes. And every animal means different character. You same as my girl, born in Year of

Dog. And Dog Year people . . . oh, my. Can be selfish. Very stubborn. But also, Dog Year people know what is right and fair." He gave her a warm smile.

"Hing," Father said, "in honour of your New Year, you may leave at noon today. And take the whole day off tomorrow."

"Thank you." Hing clasped his hands and bowed. "If I may . . . I take Em-ry to Chinese theatre tomorrow?"

"Oh, Father!" Emily exclaimed. "Please say yes!"

Her parents exchanged glances. Then Father said, "Of course. As long as Hing brings you home in time for tea."

Emily hugged herself with excitement. Tomorrow, the theatre. And today, Chinese New Year!

Hundreds of people turned out for the celebration. Chinatown echoed with the clash of cymbals and the bursting of firecrackers. Bright-red banners flew from shop windows. Enormous paper lanterns dangled from balconies and lamp-posts. Wealthy merchants, dressed in their finest silks, offered wine, nuts, and fruit to the visitors who stopped by their shops. Emily's family received one warm welcome after another.

Every merchant gave each of the girls a small red envelope containing a five-cent piece. "*Lai see*," one merchant explained. "Lucky money. The more we give away, the more luck we get. It's a tradition."

Emily thought it was a grand idea. She waved to two Chinese children clutching their *lai see* envelopes and called out, "*Gung hey fat choy!*" The girls covered their mouths and giggled, but their mother returned Emily's greeting.

"What will you do with your lucky money, Em?" Jane asked. "I'm going to buy some new coloured pencils. May I, Father?"

"Certainly."

"I'm going to buy a pony," said Amelia.

"It will have to be a very small pony." Father chuckled. "How about you, Emily?"

"I'll put it in my new bank account. And save it up for a bicycle."

He looked very pleased.

The Chinese theatre was nothing like the posh Victoria Opera House. Even getting there was an adventure. Emily took Hing's hand as they walked through a maze of alleys, along a narrow passageway, and up a flight of stairs. At the top, they entered a large, dimly lit room filled with benches. One end of the room served as the stage and was set up with the strangest musical instruments Emily had ever seen. Their sounds were even stranger.

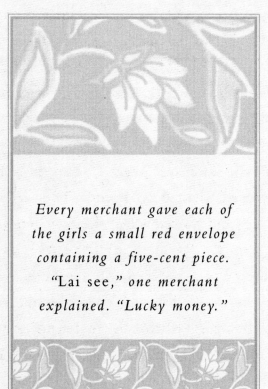

*Every merchant gave each of
the girls a small red envelope
containing a five-cent piece.
"Lai see," one merchant
explained. "Lucky money."*

The play had already started when Hing and Emily sat down, and she quickly realized that to follow the story, she had to use her imagination. When a chair was placed on the stage, for example, Hing said, "Mountain." Later, when she asked about two chairs, he said, "House." She was astonished to learn that the actors were always men. Even the women's roles were played by men speaking in high-pitched voices.

And the audience! They fell asleep, coughed and snored, chatted to friends. They stretched their legs and walked across the stage. There was even a group of men playing some kind of clicking game in the back. All this while the play was going on. And the actors didn't even mind!

The best part was that the merchants were still handing out lucky money. There weren't many children at the theatre, but those who were there, including Emily, had a growing pile of red envelopes on their laps.

She was surprised when Hing said it was time to go. "It's not over," she said.

"Play goes on and on and on," he explained. "People come and go. Now time for tea."

They left the theatre and walked out into the sunlight. It was cold and clear, a fine February day, bursting with the sound of firecrackers.

"Will your daughter have firecrackers in China?" Emily asked.

Hing smiled. "Oh, yes! Big firecrackers. Lots of noise!"

"And lucky money?"

"Not much money. Village poor. Maybe little bit."

"I could send her some of mine."

"No, no. You keep."

Half and half, Emily decided. As they walked across the James Bay bridge, she pictured Hing's little girl opening the package from Victoria and finding a *lai see* envelope filled with Canadian coins. She wouldn't be able to spend them, so she'd have to save them for when she came here. In the meantime, she'd have extra luck, and so would Emily.

She'd still save *some* of her New Year's money for a bicycle. As for the rest, Father would understand.

She gave a little skip, realizing how lucky she was that *her* father was not off in some distant land. He was just around the corner, waiting for her to come home.

*Dear Reader,*

*Did you enjoy reading this Our Canadian Girl adventure? Write us and tell us what you think! We'd love to hear about your favourite parts, which characters you like best, and even whom else you'd like to see stories about. Maybe you'd like to read an adventure with one of Our Canadian Girls that happened in your hometown—fifty, a hundred years ago or more!*

**Send your letters to:**

Our Canadian Girl
c/o Penguin Canada
10 Alcorn Avenue, Suite 300
Toronto, ON  M4V 3B2

*Be sure to check your bookstore for more books in the Our Canadian Girl series. There are some ready for you right now, and more are on their way.*

*We look forward to hearing from you!*

*Sincerely,*
  *Barbara Berson*
  PENGUIN BOOKS CANADA

*P.S. Don't forget to visit us online at www.ourcanadiangirl.ca—there are some other girls you should meet!*

*Canada's*

**1608**
Samuel de
Champlain
establishes
the first
fortified
trading post
at Quebec.

**1759**
The British
defeat the
French in
the Battle
of the
Plains of
Abraham.

**1812**
The United
States
declares war
against
Canada.

**1845**
The expedition of
Sir John Franklin
to the Arctic ends
when the ship is
frozen in the pack
ice; the fate of its
crew remains a
mystery.

**1869**
Louis Riel
leads his
Métis
followers in
the Red
River
Rebellion.

**1871**
British
Columbia
joins
Canada.

**1755**
The British
expel the
entire French
population
of Acadia
(today's
Maritime
provinces),
sending
them into
exile.

**1776**
The 13
Colonies
revolt
against
Britain, and
the Loyalists
flee to
Canada.

**1837**
Calling for
responsible
government, the
Patriotes, following
Louis-Joseph
Papineau, rebel in
Lower Canada;
William Lyon
Mackenzie leads the
uprising in Upper
Canada.

**1867**
New
Brunswick,
Nova Scotia
and the United
Province of
Canada come
together in
Confederation
to form the
Dominion of
Canada.

**1870**
Manitoba joins
Canada. The
Northwest
Territories
become an
official
territory of
Canada.

**1783**
Rachel

# *Timeline*

**1885**
At Craigellachie, British Columbia, the last spike is driven to complete the building of the Canadian Pacific Railway.

**1898**
The Yukon Territory becomes an official territory of Canada.

**1914**
Britain declares war on Germany, and Canada, because of its ties to Britain, is at war too.

**1918**
As a result of the Wartime Elections Act, the women of Canada are given the right to vote in federal elections.

**1945**
World War II ends conclusively with the dropping of atomic bombs on Hiroshima and Nagasaki.

**1873**
Prince Edward Island joins Canada.

**1896**
Gold is discovered on Bonanza Creek, a tributary of the Klondike River.

**1905**
Alberta and Saskatchewan join Canada.

**1917**
In the Halifax harbour, two ships collide, causing an explosion that leaves more than 1,600 dead and 9,000 injured.

**1939**
Canada declares war on Germany seven days after war is declared by Britain and France.

**1949**
Newfoundland, under the leadership of Joey Smallwood, joins Canada.

**1896**
Emily

**1885**
Marie-Claire

**1917**
Penelope

# Don't miss your chance to meet all the girls in the Our Canadian Girl series...

The story takes place in Montreal, during the smallpox epidemic of 1885. Marie-Claire, who lives in a humble home with her working-class family, must struggle to persevere through the illness of her cousin Lucille and the work-related injury of her father – even to endure the death of a loved one. All the while, Marie-Claire holds out hope for the future.

The year is 1917. Penny and her little sisters, Emily and Maggie, live with their father in a small house in Halifax. On the morning of December 6, Penny's father is at work, leaving Penny to get her sisters ready for the day. It is then that a catastrophic explosion rocks Halifax.

Ten-year-old Rachel arrives in northern Nova Scotia in 1783 with her mother, where they reunite with Rachel's stepfather after escaping slavery in South Carolina. Their joy at gaining freedom in a safe new home is dashed when they arrive, for the land they are given is barren and they don't have enough to eat. How will they survive?

# Watch for more Canadian girls in 2002...

Penguin Books Canada Ltd. • www.ourcanadiangirl.ca